Mike & Alex, the Defenders of the Animal Forest

Mike & Alex, Volume 1

Peter van Wermeskerken

Published by Peter van Wermeskerken, 2023.

This is a work of fiction. Similarities to real people, places, or events are entirely coincidental.

MIKE & ALEX, THE DEFENDERS OF THE ANIMAL FOREST

First edition. October 3, 2023.

Copyright © 2023 Peter van Wermeskerken.

ISBN: 979-8224711109

Written by Peter van Wermeskerken.

Table of Contents

Mike & Alex

1

The Defenders of the Animal Forest

by Peter van Wermeskerken

~* ~* ~* ~

Smashwords License Notes

~ * ~ * ~ * ~

Contact the Author via email: broervanpaul@gmail.com

CHAPTER 1:

Mike the Rabbit and Alex the Swine

His mother called him Michael, along with some more siblings, when he was born. Mike was the most active of all the young bunnies. He played with his brothers and sisters in the forest, skipping, running, and digging, which they learned from their mom and dad. 'Catch-me-as-you-can' was also a good game, especially if you were chased. The trick was to let the follower come so close he almost had you and then suddenly jump a corner to a tree. Usually, the follower went right through, and if he dared to jump, he had to be careful not to bump into the hard tree.

"Yes," Mike called when his mother yelled for him. He and his siblings had an excellent life in the forest. There were also other animals to play with. As for foxes, cats, and ferrets, they had to be careful. Mike's best friend was Alexander, the small swine.

Alexander also had many brothers and sisters, but Alex was the smallest of all. He wasn't as strong as the others and always got pushed away from the food. When they played, he almost always lost. His brother and sisters were more robust and faster. Besides Mike, Alex was more excellent.

The little swine and the giant rabbit liked to play together in the farmer's cornfield. But once, that nasty farmer sent his vicious dog Mason into the cornfield. "Get out, you!" the dog threatened as he repeatedly barked, running towards them. The dog paused and gasped. That darned rabbit jumped beside him, and so he lost sight of the swine. Now, he had to go snooping for a track, which would take much longer. "My boss doesn't want you digging holes in his cornfield. I'll keep watch," barked the dog.

Alex and Mike gathered enough courage to go cautiously to the cornfield's edge a few days later. They did not see Mason, and Mike's sniffing nose could not smell him either. On a good day, Mike proposed to Alex to go along the cornfield's edge that night. "Let's have an afternoon nap so we'll be awake at night," he said. That night, they walked along the cornfield, cautious in case the dog jumped out.

"Does a dog need to sleep, just like us?" Mike asked his friend. "I think so," Alex had growled. "He's an animal like us."

Mike and Alex were now grown-up children among pigs and rabbits. They already felt massive; therefore, they were daring and wanted to explore the world. When they arrived at the corner of the field, in the deep twilight, they saw the farmhouse and an old, large barn with several doors. The rear door in that row, which was closest to them, was slightly open. Gently, it squeaked back and forth in the light evening breeze.

Mike and Alex were curious. Even softer than before and very good-looking, the friends approached, creeping. They sniffed at all kinds of odors that they did not know. They wondered whether they should feel afraid, but their curiosity overcame them. They had promised to continue to help each other. And together, they were strong.

Near the stable, Mike sniffed once more. He smelled the dog and other animals, including cows and pigs. Mike hopped quickly to the door. He jumped inside, rushing when a more brutal gust threatened to clamp the door shut. Fortunately, the door did not fall into the lock. Alex had seen his friend inside jumping, but he was too big to slip inside. With his sturdy body, he had to give a little push to the boards of the fence of the barn. The boards broke quickly.

Mason heard that creaking sound! The dog rushed out of his cage, furious and shouting. "What are you doing here? I'm the boss here." Alex was scared, but he did what his father had taught him. He braced himself. He lowered his head slightly to give the rapidly approaching dog a fierce poke with his complex nose.

Oops! The long, thick rope that functioned as the lead for the dog was too short! Suddenly, the rope cut into his neck. Instead of catching his prey, he flew onto his back. Ouch!!

The dog scrambled up and, dazzled, he looked in the direction where Alex had just stood. But the door had blown open wide enough for the wild swine to follow his friend inside quickly.

Alex heard a soft slurping when he had settled his emotions of fear for the dog. Meanwhile, his eyes became accustomed to the darkness. His nose smelled something very familiar. He saw it, too: a large sow with her children was on the floor. "Welcome," grunted the large mother pig, "Do I get companionship?"

"Are you a pig, just like me?" Alex asked

"Come to my front so I can see you better," growled the pig on the ground with the high tone of a female.

Alex walked to her front, taking care not to tread on all those cute little piglets.

"I've seen you. We look very much alike. We're like family, but you have bigger teeth and brown skin with black lines. We have smaller teeth, and our skin is white."

"Are these your children?" Alex asked

"Yes, those are my piglets, my baby pigs."

"So you're a pig, and they are your baby pigs? What's your name?"

"Yes, I'm a pig, and the farmer calls me sow Sophie. A sow is a mother pig."

"You know a lot, Sophie; I'm Alex. Have you seen my boyfriend, Mike?

"You mean that little skipper, who is smaller than my piglets? You can hear him slurping. He said he was hungry, and I told him he could eat my leftovers."

Alex suddenly felt terrible, and his stomach growled.

"Sophie, do you think there is something for me? You must have enough food to feed all your piglets."

"You're a sweetheart," Sophie said. "There is enough, and the farmer always gives me too much. It tastes good, but I want to remain a real pig lady, slim enough not to be slaughtered this autumn. Come here; I want to smell your nose."

Alex did so. Sophie pulled her face back and said, "Go ahead, my boy."

Boy, that was good! That meal was a feast for Alex. "Sophie," he said between his slobbering, "You have delicious food!"

"Eat it and keep feasting. That's good for a young pig like you, as it will make you bigger and stronger. What do you eat where you come from?"

Alex paused his slobbering and licked his mouth. "I eat in the forest, which is behind the cornfield. We eat the soft parts of roots."

"That's far, then you've made a long and tiring walk," said Sophie.

" I'm used to long walks," said Alex. Sometimes, I run fast because of a dog or other animal."

Sophie had to laugh: "That's Mason. He makes a lot of noise, but he's harmless. He can't even properly growl. Mason has a small heart. You can walk up to him and talk to him. He won't bite."

"Well, thank you, Sophie. I have some leftover food for you. I think Mike also has his fill now."

The rabbit was already waiting. He said, "Yes, that was tasty!"

"Alex, it's unnecessary to leave me any food," said Sophie. "Every day, the farmer brings me too much food. He thinks I need so much for my piglets, but I try to teach them to eat, not just to drink with me."

Alex continued drooling until he had eaten all of Sophie's food.

Mike and Alex said in unison, "Thank you, dear Mama Sophie; that was tasty!"

Sophie said: "Well done, guys, now go back to sleep."

"Dear Mrs. Sophie," said Mike, "I think our fathers and mothers are already worried. Perhaps we are angry because we ran away together and aren't safe at home. And I think it's now dark outside."

"Well, then go home now," said Sophie. "I only tell Mason, and he won't tell anyone else. But you have to promise me one thing first. No more animals should come here from out of the woods. With the two of you, I find it cozy enough."

"Yes, Mom Sophie, we promise," said Mike and Alex.

Mama Sophie, who had experience raising pigs, knew she had to tell her children what was allowed and what wasn't. Later, they would want to explore and see what they could do and what was too dangerous.

"Mason!" cried Sophie, standing up. "I've told the rabbit and swine to go home now. You don't need to worry." And to the youngsters, she said, "I hope to see you again soon. That was fun!"

"Thank you, dear Mama Sophie," shouted Alex and Mike. "We'll be back soon." Alex cried as he struggled to wriggle between the broken slats.

~* ~* ~* ~

CHAPTER 2:

Mike and Alex Grow Fast

One day, Alex played with his sisters, Fonda and Emma, and his brothers, Bernard and Terence. Between the plays, they ate tasty roots in the ground. Fonda seemed to have found one. Alex rushed and threw his sister out of the way. "Look at our little Alex now!" shouted Terence. He had not noticed Alex had grown so big by all his visits to sow Sophie and the excellent food of the pig farmer. To his surprise, Alex did not fall and was confident against his former big brother.

"What were you thinking, Terence? I grow too!" said Alex, smiling from ear to ear.

"Alex has always been the smallest of us. You could easily push him aside," said Bernard.

"Yes," Emma said. "We all know that, Bernard. But our brother is now almost as big as all of us, and he's, in any case, thicker. See what a nice belly. "She stroked her muzzle affectionately on Alex's stomach. He grunted with pleasure.

"Shall we have a game running or catching tail?" asked Fonda. "Then we can see whether Alex isn't too thick and if he's still the slowest of us. Alex, dare you?"

"Yes, I dare," said the swine. He thought of the times he had to run from Mason. Recently, first Trevor Wolf, and a few days later, Fox Liam had hunted him and Mike. Due to their clever running, they had shaken them off. With Trevor, they laughed. The wolf ran faster, but Alex and Mike had run on the jetty when they came to the forest lake. There

...sow Sophie likes her visitors...

were two rowing boats. Mike had jumped into the first and made the second loose. Alex just about managed to jump into the boat with Mike. But Trevor jumped into the second boat, and because of its speed and weight, the wolf quickly drove onto the lake. Trevor cried with anger as he drove away with an empty stomach, all alone, and a painful lump on his head. He had bumped it against a bench. Alex grinned once more.

"Well, are you still doing it?" called Bernard, who had the longest legs and whose left front leg had already drawn a starting line.

Alex went to stand in between Terence and Bernard. He found the game with the boys exciting. Previously, the girls had also been faster than him, but he thought he'd now win. Bernard counted down: "One, two, and a half."He took a step. "And three. "The biggest swine with the longest legs took the lead with a slight edge. But Alex had run more than the others. Therefore, he was better trained and could speed up when they were halfway. The girls came behind, and the catch-up to Terence was converted into a slight lead. He came closer to Bernard.

The other animals in the forest shook their heads when they saw the young wild boars running. The rabbits encouraged Alex. "Should I call?" asked the calf of a roe to her mother. "No, honey, that's unnecessary, and we must behave ourselves. We're the noble animals of the woods."

"But we will call for the girls who are behind?"

"Yes, that's good," Mom said. The calf yelled out loud, "Fonda! Emma! Faster!!!"

All the animals encouraged one of the swine, which sounded like music to Alex's ears. It gave him extra energy, and slowly but surely, he overtook Bernard. Bernard was so tired that Terence also defeated him. The smiling girls ran over the finish line together.

"You're almost a real male wild swine," Emma told her brother. Alex almost told her that it was because he and Mike went to see Sophie every evening. But just in time, he realized he'd promised not to tell. "Yes, dear sister, that's because we're taught wise lessons from the animals off the farm."

Mike had also grown strong lately. Playing with his brothers and sisters wasn't fun anymore. During the day, he set off with his father, demanding more speed and power, but he was now more remarkable than his father. He learned from his Dad that if you stood on each other's backs, you could look much further and smell sharper. Together, they trained that way.

"Mike," Father William had told him, "Explain why you and Alex have grown so much lately?"

"Well, Dad," said Mike. That's because..."He stopped to check if he could make something up or whether it was better to tell the truth. His mother, Isabella, had taught him never to lie. But he remembered Sophie's words.

"Well, Dad, that's because," repeated the young rabbit.

Dad smiled. "Come on, boy, come with me to the thread. But don't lie." He understood his son fought a fight. "Don't be afraid. Fathers and mothers always love their children."

Mike crept closer to his father in the tuber fields. Before he went to tell him, he took a bite out of a turnip for him. Mike turned his full mouth to Dad's big ear. He flinched. "Do not talk with your mouth full in my ear! That can only hear well if no saliva and turnips are in it." They both laughed.

Mike quickly ate so that now his mouth was empty. "I'll tell you, but you must promise not to pass it on to the other rabbits, Mom, and my brothers and sisters." "I promise," Father William said.

"Well, it's like this. Alex and I often played in the cornfield. There, we met Mason, the dog of the peasant. At first, he wasn't so nice, but later he invited us there. One evening on the farm, he brought us into Sophie's loft. Sophie is a pig. She looks like a swine, but she says she's a pig. Sophie receives a lot of food from the peasants daily, more than she needs. Every night, Sophie asked us to eat the food she had left. And it tastes delicious!"

"Now I understand," said the father. "Sophie is a smart pig. A pig and a swine are almost the same, but not quite. Sophie wants to get older and remain healthy; consequently, she's slim. She doesn't overeat, but enough. The farmer wants to make her fat and slaughter her. Then, the humans will kill her. They do this with thunderous bangs. Always be careful of people with bang pipes."

"Listen to me carefully, Mike. I don't forbid you to go to Mason and Sophie. But remember that we're in the woods and on the field. Diseases from the farm could ruin our lives, or you could make the animals on the farm sick. You can discuss that with Sophie, but you better not touch her. Stay away if you ever have a cold or Sophie has a cold."

"Dad, I understand that. May I talk about that with Alex?"

"Of course, boy."

That evening, Alex and Mike met again at the familiar place at the small dam across the ditch. "We're now big and strong," said Alex, describing his race. Then Mike told about the conversation with his father.

The two teenagers found what Father William had said to be wise. So they decided to follow his advice. That night, they talked about it with Sophie. The mother pig looked a little sad. "Will you continue to come here? It's so nice to chat with you. Today, the farmer took my piglets and put them into another cage. That's no fun for a mother, although I can still hear them."

"You don't have any other piglets to care for?" asked Mike.

Now Sophie had to laugh. "The piglets grow in the womb of a mother. The farmer always decides which sow goes to the bear. The bear is the male pig. He jumps on your back, and then the piglets are born sometime later. It's so nice when they all are healthy and lie against your belly. I must, therefore, ensure that the farmer goes with me to the bear and not with another sow. Therefore, I must be in good condition and not greasy."

Mason joined them. "I admire the good condition of the forest animals. These two are skinny, but they can run fast. More movement would also be good for you, Sophie."

On a proposal from Sophie, they all danced through the pigpen in the thick straw.

The following day, the farmer found Mason and Sophie dancing and having fun in the yard. He laughed, especially when the two animals looked at him and then at each other with love in their eyes. He crouched down and put his arm around the thick neck of the mother pig. "So, sow Sophie, will you go back to the bear? It looks like you're doing your best to be in excellent condition to qualify for the next litter of piglets."

Sophie smiled and gleamed. "Yes, dear farmer, I'd like that very much," growled Sophie. The farmer did not understand her, but Mason translated to Jack the horse. The farmer could understand the old horse.

From now on, Sophie was allowed to walk freely across the yard, sometimes dancing and sometimes running with Mason. She could walk in the orchard and root around after she had promised not to destroy the roots of farmer Jacob's fruit trees. He promised to fill a feeding tube for Alex and Mike every evening.

~* ~* ~* ~

PETER VAN WERMESKERKEN

...the brothers and sisters wild boar at the start of their run...

CHAPTER 3:

A Stranger on the Farm Next Door

On the farm next to that of farmer Jacob and his wife Carla, where other people had come to live. Was that fluff? Jacob had told Jack, his horse, which he described as the most handsome of all animals, that the farmhouse was sold to people from the city.

Jack had asked his farmer why he had not bought it. "I don't want nor need the old buildings. The other neighbor, Francisco, and I have each bought half of his cows, and we rent part of his pasture. If Steve and Marie die, Francisco and I will buy the land. The farmhouse has been sold to people from the city," the farmer replied. "They are called Baron and Baroness Brilliance d'Appearance till NothingintheMain, and they have one daughter."

Jacob now had many more cows, so more calves would be born in the first months of the new year. Jack told Emily, the leader of the cows, that They walked in the same pasture. "Oh, dear!" Emily had said. "If more cows come, I might have to defend my position as the herd leader."

Emily was worried. She had no desire to fight for leadership at her age. But the cows she now leads would expect a fight from her.

The introduction of the new cows came earlier than expected. Jacob took his half of the cows the next day. The two herds were introduced. Now came the big moment for Emily. "I lead my flock here on this land. We are now one big herd. Do you all accept me as your leader?"

An unordered discussion arose between the mooing cows. The farmers, Jacob and Steef, watched from the fence. Jack acted as chairman. "Order!" he whinnied loudly. "Which of the newbies wants to say something to Emily? Emily is eight years old and has the experience and wisdom to lead a herd. If you are younger than seven years, it makes no sense to challenge Emily."

The older cows from the new, smaller herd did not want the problems Emily had as a leader. From the younger ones, one stepped forward. Jack came to her. "What's your name?" he asked gently.

"I have the most beautiful name. My name is Marianne."

"You're still young, as I can see. You're so pretty in your skin," said Jack. "It would be a shame if your skin was damaged. Through a fight, that can happen, and it hurts, too."

"Jack," said Marianne, "I like you, but I want to achieve something in life." Proudly, she stood before him.

"Marianne," said the wise horse. "In France, you're special. But here, all grown-up cows are common and have the same rights and duties." Marianne looked glum and then retreated.

The two farmers looked amused at the scene. "That Marianne is a special cow," said Steve in the accent in his area, taking a firm pull of his cigar. "Yes, I see," replied Jacob.

There began a period of activity at the three farms. Jacob built a new stall barn for his cows. The cows could walk in and out throughout the year and lie in the straw. At the end stood the milk duct. Eight cows were milked simultaneously with milking machines, handled by Jacob and Carla.

Francisco and Jacob helped each other because they wanted a dam in the ditches between their lands and that of old Steef. They laid a big concrete tube on the bottom of each ditch because the water in the ditch had to flow. Trucks drove on and off at the three farms, taking rubble and building materials to a demolition company and building materials. When the dams were finished, they mowed the long grass upon the pastures of Steef. That grass was dried in the sun to make hay to feed the cows in the winter.

That was like marshmallow to the snout of the swallows! They flew over the dry grass. Sometimes sharp right, then up and to the left. At every turn, they nibbled an insect from the air. And there were so many! Pete and Olivia sat down to rest on the back of a cow. They had gotten hot in the bright sunshine. Therefore, they wanted to fly to the forest lake and bathe in a shallow spot.

When Pete and Olivia came a few days later, they looked mad when they saw all the tiles thrown down from the roof. "Great news, great news!" cried Ryan, the cock dove and man of Dora. "There's a load of reeds." That made Pete and Olivia happy. Insects permanently settle in the thick layer of thatch on a roof.

Demolishers had come to the old, long barn where the chickens and pigs had lived. Behind the farmhouse, there was a big hole that had been dug in the ground. There was a concrete floor, and the walls were tiled, like the surrounding terrace. In the end, there was also water. Significantly, very early in the morning, the Duck family went to swim there. Even before they landed in the water, they felt the prick in their noses. "Pfffbrrr, leave here! This isn't healthy," quacked Dad, who flew away immediately, followed by his wife and children.

They landed on the heath. "Shoot, you stink," cried a moorhen. "At a farm now under reconstruction, they have a pond with obvious water, but that's not right," Father Duck quacked. He took another deep dive into the forest lake and continued for as long as a duck can stay underwater. He came up again, splashing with his wings. His wife and children did the same. They would never again go to that clear pond.

The vegetable garden of farmer Steve was transformed into a beautiful lawn. That made the moles happy. Farmer Steef had the vegetable garden fertilized with plant remains and never used poison. So many worms and beetles in the soil were tasty to the moles. Courtney and John went to try the soil beneath the lawn one night. Delighted, they returned. Courtney was pregnant, and she would be able to raise a giant nest of baby moles.

That was easier said than done. Shortly after the moles had established themselves on the lawn, a few corridors collapsed. This meant that new corridors would have to be dug. John looked carefully over the ground. It was dark, under a large wooden deck. In the distance, he saw where the platform ended.

"Courtney, dear, the townspeople all have boards laid on their pasture. I'm afraid they're up to something unhealthy for us. Let's go back to the pasture next door and hear what the other animals know to tell us." His wife agreed because she wanted her children to be at peace.

Once back in the pasture, John stuck his head above the grass again and saw a sheep named Sarah. "Do you know why those people have made all the wood on their turf that hinders our digging in the corridors?"

"Yes bahè, bahè, bahè" the sheep bleated. "They will welcome their new home with loud music and people. If we can, we'll run, but that's easier for you."

"Yes, and Courtney is pregnant," said John.

"Then go as far away as you can. An expectant mother should rest," said Sarah.

"Is it not safe enough?" asked John.

"According to Jack, the horse, even the ground, will soon pound with noise."

John thanked Sarah and told his wife everything. They left that same day and settled in many pastures away. The news spread throughout the forest. The animals gathered at the pasture's edge so Jack and the cows could talk. Alex ran to Sophie occasionally to hear her opinion.

At that time, Sophie had no piglets. She looked longingly at farmer Jacob, who watched how the animals gathered at the end of his land. "Yes, Sophie, go," he said, opening the gate to her yard. The farmer laughed as he watched his pig trot behind the well-trained Alex.

When Sophie heard what it was, the shock hit her heart. Two other sows in the pig barn had given birth to piglets. So there were now many very young and inexperienced piglets, with two of the youngest sows. The noise Jack spoke about would put them all under tremendous stress, and bad things would happen.

Sophie sent Alex to the stable for Melissa and Heather to prepare. She asked Jack if he wanted to talk to Jacob. Jack did. And do you know what? Jacob had a fantastic plan.

The farmer said, "Jack, tell Sophie she has to go to the loft between Heather and Melissa's sows. I'll open the little doors between these lofts. Sophie has to calm down the two other sows and save the piglets. The sows have one day to trust each other."

He continued, "Tell the swine, deer, cows, and other larger animals to come with me tonight on the farm. I will put on some good food for all. We've got to talk about my plan. I'll open the gate on the cows dam between their farm and mine. When I give the signal, you'll run over to the dam and the duckboards around the farm and then return to my yard."

Jack thanked his boss. Also, several smaller animals yelled, "We want to join!" and Emily, the herd leader, roared. All the cows voted loudly. Jacob understood. Like Father Wolf and his three sons, Liam and his family saw the fun of it: hunting the people!

"Nice!, Nice!, Nice!" cried Father Wolf. "Liam, I'm sure the people will be afraid of me, you and the swine!"

Mr. Owl warned, "Dear animals, love it; let the people be scared, but make sure no one gets hurt by us."A calm Emily said, "Mr. Owl, we would like to, but we cows aren't as agile as the foxes and wolves. If someone is suddenly right in front of me, my natural reaction is to put my head down and throw the human aside with my horns, and when I run, I cannot stop so easily."

Mr. Owl said, "If that happens, it'll be bad luck for that man. I'll ask the cows to overthrow the posts with those lamps and big black boxes. From those big boxes comes the worst sound."Now, the cows had a particular task! But foremost, they had one more night to sleep. Many animals could not get to sleep as usual. They were excited about their role in ruining the party of the townspeople.

The first partygoers arrived with their cars early in the afternoon on the day of the festivities. When all the parking spaces in the city were total, cars could be parked at Farmer Jacob's. For those people, he opened the gate of the dam. The guests were drinking, eating snacks, swimming, or chatting. The weather was beautiful.

"Music! We want music!" someone shouted. The music was turned on. It was not the noise that farmer Jacob and the animals had feared. It was pleasant, harmonious music. But first, everybody was invited to a buffet. The guests could fill their plates with excellent food, ranging from burgers to oysters, caviar, and chips. The drinks varied from cola to champagne. They were either inside, sitting in the former cow stable at round tables, or outside by the pool.

After coffee, almost all the younger guests went to the platform in front. DJ Stevie had brought everything: additional amplifiers, microphones, and an installation with round little mirrors in which light of all colors flashed.

Suddenly, there was a wall of sound blaring from the enormous speakers. The watching pigeons nearly fell from the tree branches and flew away. Mr. Owl watched. "How uncivilized is that noise?" he said to his wife. But she didn't hear him. Due to the flashing lights, they had to close their eyes. The couple wanted to study the reactions of the people. The animals came running.

The first was unexpected: the Rat family still stayed on the old farm of farmer Steef. The deer ran over the dam a little ahead of the other animals. They ran in a group of twenty or so, gracefully avoiding all obstacles over the platform.

There were the foxes and wolves! And there were the screaming people! "Another round, this is fun!" Father Wolf told Liam. One of the Wolf sons slipped at the pool and splashed in where people had sought a safe bath. They didn't know how fast to get out and into the barn that offered refuge. The little wolf was not yet a good swimmer, but his father hoisted him by his neck from the stinking water.

Now followed the swine, followed by farmer Jacob's two horses and cattle. The installation of the DJ was trampled. The otherwise macho DJ left a river of tears when he saw this from a safe distance inside the farmhouse. Some cows were caught up in the party ribbons. Everything else was pulled down. When the foxes and wolves came for the second time, there was little work to be done. The people were gone as they had fled into the old farmhouse through the door and open windows.

Once back at Jacob's farm, there was laughter on all sides. Jacob smiled after Jack told them what had happened with the young wolf. "We'll wash him well," said Carla energetically. "Don't use soap, just lukewarm and cold water," her husband replied.

Trevor ordered his son to remain out at the pump. Carla picked him up. He wanted to bite, but Trevor called in time, "Off." A bucket of lukewarm water was poured over his head. Carla let him lean on her left arm and pumped water over him with her right. Brrr!! What was that c-c-cold?! After a few buckets of lukewarm water, Carla put him in the pump box on his four legs. She gave him a water massage on his stomach. A bucket of lukewarm water, which was also massaged, came over his back. Then his tail. He did not like massages under his tail, but he had to surrender. Suddenly, the little wolf was lifted out of the water. He saw nothing. "Dad!" he cried. Father Trevor was in stitches. A big towel had swallowed the little wolf, and Carla and Jacob rubbed the hair of the wolf kid dry. When the towel was gone, he jumped at Carla and licked her hand, wagging his tail.

"Your wife has a new boyfriend," Jack grinned at the farmer. The animal clippers burst into laughter until an angry neighbor appeared in the doorway.

"Come on, girls!" said Emily. The cows formed a front and slowly drove the man to his yard. From a distance, he dared to curse...

~* ~* ~* ~

...Horse Jack Makes Peace Among the Cows...

CHAPTER 4:

Protest Against Construction Car-Path

The Big Animal Forest consists of two parts: the left forest and the right forest. The left forest ends at a stream through the valley. The right forest is bigger. In the middle is a bike path. Because there are so many tall trees, sunlight never shines through, called the 'dark path.' The bike path goes over the top of the hill, diagonally right toward the start of a ridge.

There is a village diagonally left in the valley, along the stream. If you go from the town and follow the bike path through the forest, you come to the 'high village' as the animals call it. That is a collection of farms, a little church, a café, and a shop where they sell everything from food to tractor tires and postage stamps to laptops. One of the farmers sells and repairs bikes, and his wife sells gasoline for cars and diesel for tractors.

The bike path is quiet. In the summer, there are twenty cyclists a day, but in the winter, the number of cyclists and moped riders is deficient. The animals have never seen cars. The birds sometimes talk about cars. They say they are terrible things. Some are noisy, some are fast, and others drive slower than the birds. Sometimes, birds or other animals are dead on the road. The family Swan saw how a big father swine wanted to defend his family. He had to pay for that with his death. Other birds had seen dead swine and deer on the verge.

No cars should be near. From her safe altitude, the young falcon girl, Abigail, had seen a long, wide stripe of white sand between the town and the high village, directed to the bike path through the forest. There were also big cars and yellow machines.

She had asked her brother Charles to join. Together, they watched and made some nosedives. They told me about it at the lake.

One night, when there was very little moonlight, Liam and his family walked along the 'high village' at a safe distance. Many trees had a red cross or a white circle. They went to get a closer look.

They saw trees with a red cross on the ground. "That's it!" Liam whispered to his wife. "The trees with a red cross shall be cut down, and those that remain will have a white circle."

"You're so handsome, sweet man, love. Explain!" said Madison, his wife, and she looked in love at Liam.

Father Fox glowed with pride. With his thick, bushy tail up, he went for his family. When Madison noticed, she ran forward. "Put down that tail! You betray us!" she hissed fiercely in his ear. Liam froze, with his tail between his legs, then dropped it slowly. The children and Madison followed. "Oh, oops! Don't be overconfident, boy," Liam thought to himself. "I must lead by example and always be careful."

The next day, the Fox family reported back, strengthened by the two chickens they had stolen from a farm. They talked about the trees on the ground with red crosses. Some had recently been cut down. "First is simply that path of white sand. We have not been there because everyone sees you, and it is quite thick. It appears that they have sharp stones under the sand. There are a few machines. Even further away, it stinks terribly. There is also machinery, and the path is black. From there, we saw that, very occasionally, there were lights on the path in the distance. The kids were tired, and we had to catch some food, so we reversed," said Liam.

His children protested but also gaped. "You need to raise your children better," said Mr. Owl. "But," he continued immediately, "That was a handy search and a clear report. Congratulations!" said the learned Mr. Owl.

Some animals began calling. "Should we move?" cried one. "What do we do now?" cried another. It was so loud that Mr. Owl could not hear well. Mike, huge now for a rabbit, jumped on the stump of a fallen tree in the last storm. "Everyone be quiet. Shut up!" he roared with the big voice of a massive rabbit. Alex interfered quickly with a few destructive animals that seemed to listen. "Grrrawl, shut up," he said threateningly. "Shut up," barked one of the young foxes to the ducks.

"The path is not going through your beautiful lake," barked the young Johnny Fox

"How do you know?" a stubborn early heron asked, who knew he did not have to be afraid of the fox. "Barking foxes don't bite, just like barking dogs," said the fox, putting his thick bushy tail up in pride. "Arch, beware that you don't lose your little tail," said the heron teasingly and hastily flew to the island when the young Mr. Fox was prepared to pounce on him.

"Fortunately, it's quiet again," said Mr. Owl. "Thank you for joining me for this, Mike, Alex and Johnny. We need a good plan. We must carry that out long before the people who make that path are in our forest. Liam, first, a question. Are there more trees to be cut down?"

"Yes, sir Owl."

"What kind of trees are they?"

"All kinds of trees, many oaks."

"That is nice," said Mr. Owl. "Like the swallows, go and see if there are caterpillars. People call them oak caterpillars. They tickle the people very, very much."

Jessica Swallow asked, "Are the caterpillars eatable?"

Mr. Owl said, "They have a lot of hair, and for people, they are poisonous."

"I'll go and watch with the family," said Jessica.

"Jessica, ask the caterpillars to go to the oaks along where the Car Path has to go. Who can talk to the ants in the woods?"

"I can," cried a young duck.

"Thank you for your willingness," said Mr. Owl. "But we have nothing for a waterbird." Disappointed, the duckling dripped away.

"Chirp, chirp, chirp," called Family Tit.

"Not all at once!" said Mr. Owl.

Father Tit gave his eldest son a slap with his wing. "We are not dangerous to the ants because we eat seeds. What do we need to ask, Mr. Owl?"

"Just ask if there are only black or red and flying ants. They can all get a job.

Brrmm, brrrm, brrrrm. A few wasps flew with Mr. Owl and landed on his branch.

"It's very friendly of you to join the army of the animals," said Mr. Owl.

"We also want to do something," they burned.

"Can you build a nest in some cars and machines in two days?

"Yes, we can. Then we swarm. Will we also ask the bees?"

"Zzzoem, zzzoem," said the wild forest bees, who had just strengthened with the honey from the flowers. We will ask our queen if she allows us to help."

"Even better," said Mr. Owl. "But we must prepare well. The people work for five days. Then they get tired and rest for two days. On those two days, we have to do everything."

Mike had his friend Alex say, "We are strong; is there still something for us to do?"

"Yes, there is quite a lot," said Mr. Owl. "Let the swine, hares, and rabbits ruffle the white sand apart. That's a lot of work."

The animals decided that Mr. Owl's plan was good. The sisters Mike, Fonda, and Emma showed the ants the path to the machines. The red ants smelt where they were needed from a distance, in the leather on the roofs of the cabins. That was expertly broken down into food with their sharp jaws. The black ants worked themselves through the most minor holes in the cabs of trucks and machines. There was still a lot of tasty, sweet food! They carried it on their backs to their nest in the forest. They had a storehouse from which they and their queen could eat throughout the winter.

The wasps and bees were divided. A swarm of wasps settled in the already broken driver seat in the cabin of a machine. A swarm of bees found beautiful places in the cabs of trucks. Where it smelled too much for the bees, spiders insisted on playing their role and built cabins full of cobwebs. Mother Webber and her daughters made a quick web, but the tar car smelled so bad that they quickly drew a wire out. Then they went quickly back to the forest.

Meanwhile, Mike and Alex had discovered a material coffin of the people. There was of everything. They called Mr. Owl.

"Oh, that's fantastic!" cried the wise general. He soon saw a giant nail. He knew it was easy to puncture a tire with a nail, but that was a sin. It turned out that Mike's brothers and sisters and the other rabbits were perfect at such a thing. This beautiful nail could be used better, thought Mr. Owl. Being the wisest couple of all animals, Mike and Alex did the deed together. The other animals were kept away from the stinking tar machine.

"Mike and Alex, first, you must open the hood here from the side."So that's what the friends did. Mike could easily reach. He tied a rope through the eye of the closure of the valve.

"Mr. Owl," Mike said, "Can you bring the rope with the nail to us as we stand on the hood?" The owl brought the nail into his claw.

Father Swine brought the requested piece of hardwood. "Now you hold the nail with a pair of pliers," Mr. Owl said as he took the pliers from the toolbox. "I hit!" cried Alex. Each thwack by big, strong Alex shook Mike's leg back. He winced. Alex hit again, and again, and again. Finally, the nail stuck a hole in the machine's gas tank. Mike almost lost his balance.

"That was beautiful. The gasoline is now dripping from the tank. Get off that hood," said Mr. Owl. That wasn't easy for Mike, as he no longer felt in his leg. Alex and his father helped him get back on the ground. His father assisted him in walking home. "Would it be good for Mike to go to Frits the Hare, the physiotherapist?" asked Emma.

"Emma, you're a good daughter of your father. And almost as handsome. Will you go with Mike to Frits?" Father Rabbit knew very well that his daughter had an eye on muscular Frits.

After the weekend, the workers returned. Their boss, Philip Roadworker, had tears in his eyes. On one of the trucks, he read, "Down with Car-Path." Jack had asked his boss to write that on the ground. Liam Fox and his family had written the words in the dirt with their feet. Philip saw that humans could not have caused this damage. He had to consider the wishes of animals; otherwise, he'd risk a repeat performance. These animals showed their willingness to fight in the woods for their autonomy. He ordered his people to repair the damage and said they would continue to build the road around the forest." He told the officials he needed more money because the road was longer.

When farmer Jacob noticed the car path had been redirected around the woods, he was happy.

"Tell the animals the road will not go through their forest, and I'll celebrate our victory in the pasture in the forest," he said to his horse Jack, who reported to Mason that he cried the news out at the edge of the cornfield. Jacob spent the next day with two bales of hay, apples and potatoes, carrots and nuts, a bag of sugar and oats, and a big feed for the best pigs in the country. "The feast is ready!" barked Mason. The animals came from the forest. Jacob looked, sitting on the fence, from a distance. He smiled. "That's what they deserve for their efforts," he thought.

Francisco later rewarded all the road workers with a package containing all kinds of cheese and fresh products of the country; a thank you for their understanding.

.....Father Fox discovers the signs on the trees...

CHAPTER 5:

The Animals Hunt the Hunters

At the end of the summer, Mike and Alex were by far the largest animals in the forest. Alex was a considerable swine, weighing over 400 pounds. If Mike stood up, he was as big as the deer. Because of their size and strength, they led the animals in the forest. They had learned a lot from farm animals: pigs, dogs, horses, cows, geese, and goats. The sheep were stupid.

From the animals in the forest, they had heard that all good periods end someday. In late summer and autumn, there was plenty to eat. Then, many animals built up large stocks for the winter. The poor cold began when the hunters came with their bangpipes and dogs. Some went to the open wooden houses on stilts at the forest's edge.

Alex and Mike met with all the animals in the forest and field. They agreed the hunting had to stop. The hunters shot animals to their deaths, but many were also wounded and suffered much pain.

With numerous other animals, Alex and Mike decided, one way or another, that they wanted to teach the hunters a lesson. They knew the hunters would walk across the field with their bangpipes over their shoulders. The dogs had to chase the animals in the forest and the fields to make it easy for the hunters to shoot them.

"We should not do anything against the hunters or also the dogs," Mike had said.

The animals had a large meeting at the edge of the forest lake. Only the pheasants were absent. Mike acted as chairman, Alex took care of the order, Mrs. Owl would write down what was agreed upon, and Mr. Owl would make a fighting plan. Liam Fox was appointed head of the Secret Service and was spying with his family at the farms in the neighborhood.

Some hunters were there early in the morning, climbing to the first twilight in a shooting house. "Yes, we should also do something against these huts. Last year, from there, they shot my dear little Natalie dead," Mom deer said.

"Can you knock over such a house?" yelled Alex and his brother Bernard. "First, you have to weaken the bottom of the pile," said Mr. Owl. "I see on the attendance list the name of William Castor."

"Wiiillllllm!" Mike shouted as loud as he could. The castor raised his head above the water further out of the fen. "Here am I," William said with a fish in his mouth.

"Rico" (that was his nickname). Mike shouted, "Can you, your wife, and children gnaw the poles of the shooting cottage by the stream so that the place where the shooting men stand falls into the water?"

".... You mean so that we may demolish the house and use the wood for our castle?"

"That seems like an excellent idea," cried Joseph, the son of Mr. and Mrs. Owl. "Shut your beak, rascal! Here, people speak only the mature way!"

Mr. Owl continued. "But there are still two shooting houses along the forest's edge. What do we do with them?"William had a proposal. "Owl!" he shouted from the water. "My family and I live in the water, especially at its edge. We are excellent rodents, but rabbits and hares are also good with their teeth. Ask them to gnaw the legs of the shooting houses and the swine to give the final push."

"Good idea, good idea," cried the crowd, including the rabbits and hares. William glowed with pride and smiled at his wife, Mina.

"Quààààk," Bas the duck called. "Then it's more enjoyable and safer for us. "He received no answer, as the other animals found the duck pretty stupid and only thinking about himself and his family.

Suddenly, there was a very slight beep. The worm stuck his head above the ground. One of the hedgehogs immediately wanted some snacks to munch, but Mr. Owl said, "Let's tell the worm, stinging hedgehog," and he cried.

"I have to broadcast what you have to say," said the hedgehog to the worm, whose head was already almost underground. "You will not eat me?" asked the worm carefully. "No, say what you have to say. I have Mr. Owl to obey."

"Well," squeaked the worm, "I want to ask if we may chew our way through the poles on the ground. Together with some beetles and insects, we can entertain, and the people cannot use the wood anymore. Moreover, it's a lot of food for us and our children."

"Splendid idea," cried Mama Deer. So, the animals decided to demolish the houses. Everyone got a task that night at work. It was raining. The animals did not bother. It would also deter people from coming to the forest.

The castors had two nights and two early mornings to knock down the hut by the stream. When the hut fell, the ladder broke away quickly. Terence and Bernard helped to bring the wood to the castle. At the downing of the other two houses, the hares and rabbits worked in four teams, each for three hours twice a day.

One morning, a few weeks later, Liam and his family were disturbed when they tried to rob a chicken at a farm. They made a noise, and quickly, they slipped away. Along the way, they hid in a wooded bank along a path. The shock hit them. There were two hunters with bangpipes. As fast as they could, they ran to the forest. Breathless, they were told that there were hunters.

At a safe distance, the deer were called off the field and told to go to the island through the forest lake. "Look," said one hunter to another on the spot where the shooting house had been. "That's what the castors have done," said one. "Look at the gnawing traces."

"Then we'll go to a different cabin," said the first hunter. But the second cabin also lay on the ground, and the third. "That seems intentionally done. Is it possible that the animals have become smart?" asked the tallest hunter. A cow bellowed approvingly from a distance.

"Look at how fast that wood is affected by worms, woodworms, and beetles," said one of them. He picked up a piece of wood. There was no need to save it, as it had been destroyed with force. "It's not useful anymore," he concluded. "Let's go home. In about ten days, we have the dog hunting."

...de aanval van de duiven op de jagers...

CHAPTER 6 - Air Force Falcraft and Pigeonbomb

The animals knew about dog hunting. That evening, they met again at the forest lake. On the advice of Mr. Owl, an air force was created. The family Falcon would spy and signal very high in the air. The first would pour down to supposedly catch a mouse. The pigeons had to be ready from that moment on.

"Oops," the pigeons had said. The falcons always hunt us.

"No, no," said Mr. Owl, "I agreed with Grandpa Joost Falcon that we do not hunt or chase each other. We fight the hunters together."

All the pigeons that visited the forest were asked to stay and maximize the forest's Air Force. Many swallows trained the pigeons to aim their bombs strictly at the bang pipes. A second bombing from the front and side would begin before the hunters could recover from the first attack from behind. The swallows had to swarm around to impress the hunters about the massive number of birds, together with shouting crows and magpies, and to escort wounded pigeons to a safe place on the ground.

Alex had suggested that the swine from the forest would grub a strip of land. This proposal was received with cheers. About 20 meters behind the moles, hares, and rabbits had to dig empty corridors and holes. On the night before the hunting, larger animals went to the intermediate strip of land to poop and pee as much as possible. They got help from the cows and horses of farmer Jacob. Mike and Alex were permitted to open the gate.

The last defense was against the dogs. A wide row of urchins half-buried themselves. Numerous forest mice were available to attack a dog that would do something against an urchin.

The swine families had to hide in the bushes at the forest's edge. "Attack is the best defense," Mr. Owl taught the animals. "If a dog or hunter breaks, the wild swine attack immediately. Make sure the banging pipe is made of cord. Often, they have things with them that are very sharp, and they cut into your skin. Therefore, there should be an attacker on either side and hold the leg in which the gun is being held."

When the day of the hunt approached, Mason, the dog of farmer Jacob, barked around the animals that wanted to defend themselves against the hunters. As always, they would accompany their bosses, but at the same time, they would not do an excellent job hunting.

Early in the morning, the hunt began. Family Falcon sought the high sky, just below the clouds. The pigeons flew to the trees that hunters would pass. They pretended they were asleep. In the trees ahead and right on both edges of the woods, hundreds—maybe even a few thousand—birds waited.

Quiet, the dogs walked along with the hunters. They did not know what lay ahead but knew from hearsay about a super-large swine and a super-large rabbit. They were both strong, and they should stay away from them. And all the forest inhabitants would fight them. They had a clear majority.

Suddenly, behind them, a falcon dropped. It seemed he would catch a mouse. Quietly, the pigeons flew from the trees. In a wide formation, they went higher. The hunters noticed nothing, but their dogs seemed to become a little nervous.

Then, suddenly, a second falcon let himself drop just before the pigeons. That signaled the pigeons to make the sharp nosedive, as they had learned from the swallows. In the end, when they were just above the bang pipes, they let their white bombs fall from their bottoms, aimed at the pipes, and then in a very sharp curve, one half to the left and the other half to the right. What a relief for the pigeons!

The dogs heard the sound of the high rush of wind along the wings of doves. Some barked, and some put their tail between their legs. The hunters looked down at their dogs. They didn't notice the second flow of bombs, now targeting their faces. The third attack came from the right, again aimed at the exhausts, the shot cartridges, and the clothes of the hunters, immediately followed by the fourth attack from the left side.

"Dirty pigeons," scolded a hunter and focused on one of them. His rifle refused; it was dirty and wet as it was. The shot cartridges were also mixed with pigeon poop. Hunter Jaime got the total load from many angry pigeons.

Only some of the hunters managed to shoot. Focusing was not possible. Only one dove, Dora, was shot in the thigh. That hurt! However, she managed to flutter to the edge of the woods. There, the nurse swallows bothered her. Prudently, the shot pellets were stolen from her thigh with their beaks. After that, Dora felt a lot better.

"Have a little lie down quietly," squeaked Doctor Swallow. "The nurses are now dealing with all wounds to prohibit infection." When that was done, the doctor called the big pigeon cock Alfonso. "Alfonso, you should support Dora as she gets up. Then wait, and if Dora can walk again, fly with her in the woods, but stay today and tomorrow with her. And you, Dora, give that leg a little rest so everything heals properly."

Some brave hunters walked by and came to the land plowed by the animals. It wasn't easy to get through it smoothly. One of the hunters kicked his foot in an underground passage. His foot sprained, and the hunter cursed. That did not improve when he reached the slippery land full of cow dung and manure. There, many of the hunters slipped. The ridges in the soles of their boots were filled with loose clay, and now the poop...

Two hunters, in revenge, sent their dogs to the forest. One stepped into a hedgehog. Crying, he went on three legs home. The second dog had seen it. "You have won!" he barked at the animals in the forest. The hunter with the horn blew "stop hunt" when he saw the dogs returning with their tails low.

Smelly and under the white and green poop, the hunters came back to the farm, where their wives were waiting for them. They smelt too much for a kiss. "Man, you stink. Your clothes are too dirty," cried the wife of peasant Delgado disapprovingly and closed her nose with two fingers. The hunters were dirty all over. In their faces, their hair, their clothes, their boots, and their hats. "Take off your clothes in the stable. Each put his clothes, hats, and boots on a pile. You will all get a plastic bag that you can wash at home. We will fill some buckets with warm water so you can wash your faces and hands here at the stable. Sarah will immediately bring you dry, clean towels and soap."

Jaime, the fattest of the hunters, asked whether the women had already cooked the meal to celebrate the end of the hunt. The ladies looked at each other, smiled, and laughed aloud. "You were just away; you didn't shoot anything, and now you want a reward for hunting. What do you have for us, except your clothes with poop?" howled Juana with her high-pitched voice. The women said the men were allowed in the large kitchen without dirty clothes and boots. One by one, the men trickled in their underwear for coffee with a slice of cake.

The animals gathered around the forest lake. The deer had returned from the island. Mike had told them they had to hide between the bushes. The Falcon family reported about the battle with the hunters. They joked about the great victory of the animals. "It was an excellent idea of Mr. Owl's to give the birds such an important task," laughed Grandpa Joost.

"Your alerts when we had to take action worked perfectly," echoed the doves. The doves, falcons, and swallows were hungry and thirsty.

For the falcons, Mr. Owl and his family got several tasty voles. They all had one or two in their claws. The Magpies were brutally flown in a swarm to a garden center. There were abundant seeds and fruits. The pigeons got many seeds collected by the animals from the farmland. Still, other birds picked grapes and berries. "Don't overeat that fruit," warned Mr. Owl. "That can make you drunk. Then you cannot fly straight or land on a branch."

~* ~* ~* ~

CHAPTER 7

The Author, Peter van Wermeskerken

Peter van Wermeskerken was born on 12-31-1939 in Zeist, the Netherlands. He became, like his father, a journalist. At the AD in Rotterdam, the second largest Dutch daily, he was a reporter and chief economics officer. He specialized in energy and monetary economics. After his retirement, his wife encouraged him to write his first book about his experiences as a Double Agent. His second book (2015) was the children's book, Mike & Alex. His wife died (2014), but he remarried and enjoyed writing again. A series of new adventures for Mike and Alex are in the pipeline. The first of these is expected in 2024. Peter has two children.

~*~* ~* ~

CHAPTER 8

More from this Publisher

The Spy, The Wall, Two Sides

This is my story about my experiences as a double agent in the Cold War. While visiting my girlfriend in East Germany I was approached by GDR military intelligence. In Holland the Secret Service took me over. In the years that followed I saw that the Berlin Wall separated two completely different worlds. Even the Eastern spymasters did not know the life in the West. That led to idiotic discussions and orders and a good laugh at the Dutch Secret Service. https://books2read.com/u/mBJlBy

Happiness follows on Friday, the 13th.

A short story about a typical British romance: Julia has a terrible day that Friday. The heel of her shoe breaks at the station, and she falls. There's a nice guy, Trevor, who wants to help. She refuses. They travel on the same train that suddenly stops in nowhere. Together, they go further, and what they'll experience then...Subsequently, Friday comes—just the day of bright sunshine! Happiness Follows on Friday, 13th [1](smashwords.com):

---

1. https://www.smashwords.com/books/view/532849

The Knickerbocker Glory Story

I sat on a terrace and listened. At the adjacent tables sat six women in their early thirties, in a great mood, sometimes a bit noisy. Their two tables were packed with glasses, empty and full plates and bowls, and bottles. The discussion had progressed to plans for next year. I just read that. A recipe for that meal is behind the short story. https://books2read.com/u/b5BBXk

A Kid During WWII Wartime

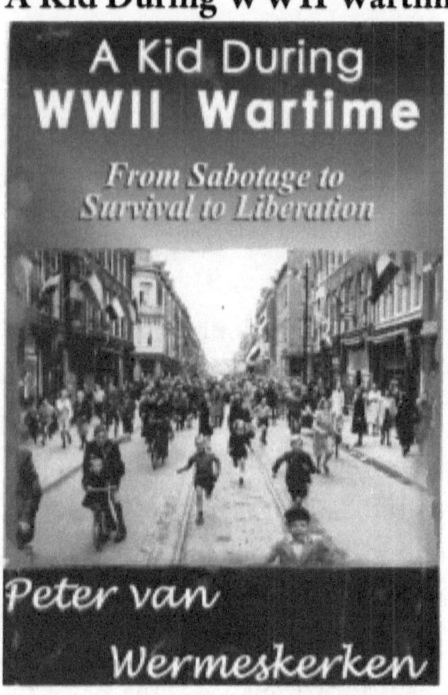

These are four stories that Peter van Wermeskerken experienced as a 4-year-old boy in the last winter of WWII. That started with sabotaging 5 German army cars on a hot day in August 1944. Furthermore, how he learned to jump the queue for the soup kitchen, I thought it was an honor to be able to go on a hunger tour. That was to get wood from the forest. The Germans did not shoot children. In May 1945, the symbol of freedom for me became a cracker with red jam. So good!

A Kid During WWII Wartime (From Sabotage to Survival to Liberation) (smashwords.com)[2]

All of my books on www.peter-s-books

Did you love *Mike & Alex, the Defenders of the Animal Forest*? Then you should read *The Spy, The Wall, Two Sides*[3] by Peter van Wermeskerken!

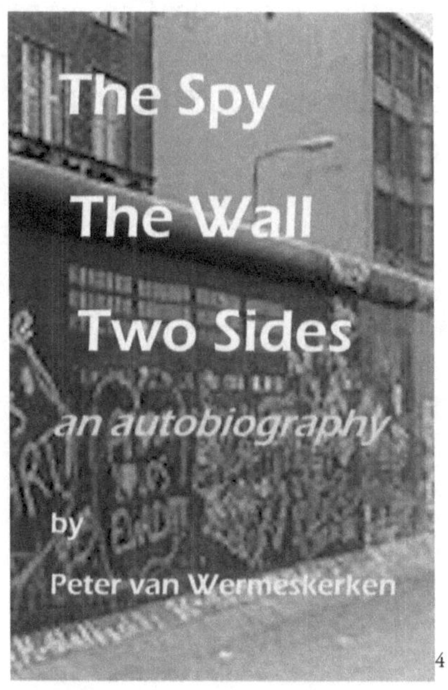

This is a revised edition of Double Agent, with the photos and biography of Margot Honecker from the first edition in 2012. I had an interview with this meanest woman in the world in her time. You can give that the motto: "How do I distort the facts." Other people (including MAGA in the USA) are now doing that again. Look after! This story is now more relevant than ever. The war in Ukraine makes it clear why NATO exists. During the Cold War, we were able to prevent a conflict due to NATO's existence. That is why it is now necessary to strengthen NATO, also on the front in Ukraine. During the Cold War, I was a double agent. That has nothing to do with adventures, and much more to do with waiting and taking endless "lessons." But you experience very strange

---

3. https://books2read.com/u/mBJlBy

4. https://books2read.com/u/mBJlBy

things. People in East Berlin had to lead me, but they had no idea how we live in the free and democratic West. That led to idiotic discussions and reactions from them when they saw my results - approved by the Dutch anti-espionage service. Essentially, I, an ordinary young journalist, defeated the Secret Service that considered itself the best in the world after Israel's Mossad. Better than the KGB and the CIA. Pride.

Read more at https://peter-s-boeken.nl.

Also by Peter van Wermeskerken

Mike & Alex
Mike & Alex, the Defenders of the Animal Forest

Standalone
The Knickerbocker Glory Story
Double Agent in the Cold War
Koffievreugd
Happiness Follows on Friday 13th
Das Glück folgt auf Freitag dem 13.
Le bonheur succède au vendredi 13
Die Geschichte des Eisbechers Knickerbocker
A Kid During WWII Wartime
Imprisoned in the Castle Ruins
The Spy, The Wall, Two Sides

Watch for more at https://peter-s-boeken.nl.

About the Author

Peter van Wermeskerken is born 12-31-1939 at Zeist, Netherlands. His father was a journalist and he followed in his footsteps. He was reporter and chef economic desk at AD daily at Rotterdam. For many years he was nr. 1 in oil reporting in the world. He studied agriculture and economics at the level of teacher Highschool. After retirement he was one period town councilor. With his first wife (deceased) he has two children. He remarried 2018. Hobbies chess and writing.

Read more at https://peter-s-boeken.nl.

www.ingramcontent.com/pod-product-compliance
Lightning Source LLC
Chambersburg PA
CBHW020330180726
47991CB00019B/1128